Picky, Picky Pete
A Boy and His Sensory Challenges

by Michele Griffin

In this book, Pete's word's will be written in RED, His mother's in PURPLE,
and the narration in BLUE. Have fun!

Picky, Picky Pete

All marketing and publishing rights guaranteed to and reserved by

1010 N. Davis Dr.
Arlington, TX 76012
Toll-free 877.775.8968
Phone 682.558.8941
Fax 682.558.8945
E-mail: info@sensoryworld.com
www.sensoryworld.com

Illustrated by Michele Griffin, OT

Printed in Canada.

ISBN 13: 978-1-935567-21-9

This book is dedicated to my family and friends who have been supportive of this project. And especially to my very own "Picky Pete", Brendan.

Picky, Picky, Picky Pete
Needed help from his Mom to stand on his feet.

"Wake up! Get dressed! And do not fuss!
Hurry up so you can catch the bus!"

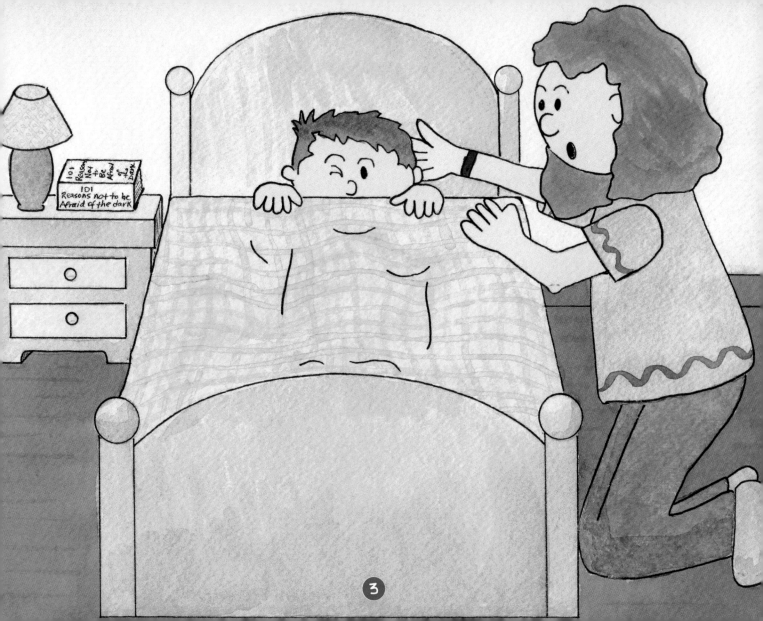

"Hurry, hurry! All the time!
I can get dressed. I'll be ready by nine!"

"Pete, let's move! Don't be a fool.
Time is ticking, and you're late for school!"

Now Pete picks out a fancy shirt.

"Wait...this one's got a little dirt."

"Hurry Peter, do not lag!"

"Hold on...this one has an itchy tag."

"My OH my. Why are you so picky?"

"Because that shirt is really itchy!"

‘Now quiet, so
can put on my
pants.”
“Oh Pete! Why are
you doing a dance?”
“These pants
are pinching at
the waist!”

"Wash my face?!
Oh no...I can't!

Just the thought
makes me start to pant!"

"Cold and gooey soap goes SPLAT!
Splashing water! I hate that!
I think that my face is really clean.
Mom, why are you being so mean?"

Now he checks his curly hair.

"Don't you comb it, don't you dare!
I like it just the way it is,
Untouched with just a little frizz."

Picky, Picky, Picky Pete
Also hated things to touch his feet.
"Put on my socks! Put on my shoes!
Grass and sand give me the blues!
But make sure that they are on just right,
Seams in place and not too tight!"

"Mom! Mom! Something's wrong.
On the left, my laces are a smidgen too long."

"Breakfast time! What will you eat?"

Nothing really interested Pete.

"I want something cold and not too sticky!"

"Pete! Why must you be so picky!"

Slowly he ate, time did linger
After each bite, the wipe of a finger.

"I'm tired...I don't want to rush."

"If you don't, you'll miss the bus!
I see it now! Here it comes!"

"Have a great day...give Mom a hug.
Remember you have art with Miss Undertug."

"Art? UGH! Finger paint?
Just the thought makes me want to faint."

"Stop being so picky, and don't start to whine! Hop on the bus, it's almost nine!"

"I'm sorry that I said you're mean,
And for all of the grouchiness in between.
I know you do so much, you see.
But being picky is part of me!"

"Mom, I am picky
Yes, that is true.
But things that bother me, don't bother you!"

"Tags, seams, and scratchy stuff,
If not 'just right' get me in a huff!
Paint, soap, and things with lumps
Make my heart and skin just jump!"

"I love you, Mom—morning, day, and night.
I am sorry when I start to fight.
When I get home I'll tell you the rest,
Remember Mom, you are the best!"

And there went Picky, Picky, Picky, Pete.
Off to school without missing a beat.

"Before you know it Pete will be back!
I'm going home to take a nap!"

To learn more about SPD:

The SPD Foundation sponsors an online site with lots of information about sensory processing disorder. There are all types of community and healthcare resources for people with sensory problems, including dentists; physicians; occupational, physical and speech-language therapists; educators; mental health professionals; eye care professionals, and community resources, such as hair salons and gymnastics programs. The site is adding community resources, such as hair salons and gymnastics programs. If you know of resources in your area, please visit this website and add them to the list.

This site also includes a link to SPD Parent Connections, a nationwide network of parent-managed community support groups for families interested in sensory processing problems.
www.SPDfoundation.net

Carol Kranowitz has a website that includes many pages of equipment, supplies, and other resources to assist people with sensory processing disorder. It also includes links to other useful sites.
www.out-of-sync-child.com

S.I. Focus magazine is the first of its kind serving as an international resource to parents and professionals who want to stay informed about sensory integration and how to address sensory processing deficits. *S.I. Focus* provides quality information written by leading people in the field as well as parents with insight into the topic.
www.SIFocus.com

Sensory World, the publisher of this book, is an imprint of Future Horizons, the world's largest publisher exclusively devoted to resources for those interested in autism spectrum disorders, Asperger syndrome, and SPD. The company also sponsors national conferences for parents, teachers, therapists, and others interested in supporting those with ASD and SPD.
www.sensoryworld.com

Additional Resources

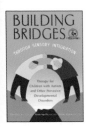

Aquilla, Paula, Yack, Ellen, & Sutton, Shirley. *Building Bridges through Sensory Integration,* 2nd ed. www.sensoryworld.com

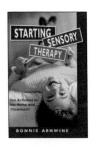

Arnwine, Bonnie (2005). *Starting Sensory Therapy: Fun Activities for the Home and Classroom!* www.sensoryworld.com

Lande, Aubrey & Wiz, Bob. *Songames™ for Sensory Integration* (CD). www.sensoryworld.com

Fisch, Marla S. *Sensitive Sam: A Sensitive Story with a Happy Ending for Parents and Kids!* www.sensoryworld.com

Grandin, Temple. *The Way I See It* and *Thinking in Pictures.* www.fhautism.com

Krzyzanowski, Joan, Angermeier, Patricia, & Keller Moir, Kristina. *Learning in Motion: 101+ Fun Classroom Activities.* www.sensoryworld.com

 Gray, Carol. *The New Social Story Book.* www.fhautism.com

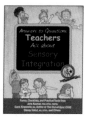 Koomar, Jane, PhD, Stacey Szklut, Carol Kranowitz, et al. *Answers to Questions Teachers Ask About Sensory Integration* (CD). www.sensoryworld.com

 Renke, Laurie, Renke, Jake, & Renke, Max. *I Like Birthdays...It's the Parties I'm Not Sure About!* www.sensoryworld.com

 Jereb, David, and Jereb, Kathy Koehler. *MoveAbout Activity Cards: Quick and Easy Sensory Activities to Help Children Refocus, Calm Down or Regain Energy.* www.sensoryworld.com

 Moyes, Rebecca. *I Need Help With School! A Guide for Parents of Children with Autism & Asperger's Syndrome.* www.FHautism.com

 Kranowitz, Carol. *The Out-of-Sync Child, 2nd ed.; The Out-of-Sync Child Has Fun, 2nd ed.; Preschool Sensory Scan for Educators (Preschool SENSE); Getting Kids in Sync* (DVD featuring the children of St. Columba's Nursery School); *The Out-of-Sync Child* (DVD); *Sensory Issues in Learning & Behavior* (DVD). www.sensoryworld.com

 Kranowitz, Carol. *The Goodenoughs Get in Sync.*
www.sensoryworld.com

 Farrington, Linda Wilson. *Squirmy Wormy.*
www.sensoryworld.com

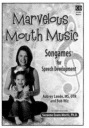 Morris, Suzanne Evans. *Marvelous Mouth Music.*
www.sensoryworld.com

 Sher, Barbara. *28 Instant Songames.*
www.sensoryworld.com

 Taylor, Kristen Fitz and McDonald, Cheryl.
Danceland.
www.sensoryworld.com

These catalog companies can provide more ideas and products for kids with Special Needs.

Abilitations
(800) 850-8602
www.abilitations.com

FlagHouse Sensory Solution
(800) 265-6900
www.FlagHouse.com

Henry Occupational Therapy Services, Inc.
(888) 371-1204
www.ateachabout.com

Integrations
(800) 622-0638
www.integrationscatalog.com

Therapro, Inc.
(800) 257-5376
www.theraproducts.com